THE RAINMAKER DANCED

THE RAINMAKER DANCED

poems by
John Agard

Pictures by
Satoshi Kitamura

Hodder
Children's
Books

HODDER CHILDREN'S BOOKS

First published in Great Britain in 2017 by Hodder and Stoughton

1 3 5 7 9 10 8 6 4 2

A CIP catalogue record for this book
is available from the British Library.

ISBN 978 1 444 93260 7

Printed and bound in Great Britain
by Clays Ltd, St Ives plc

The paper and board used in this book
are made from wood from responsible sources

MIX
Paper from
responsible sources
FSC® C104740

Hodder Children's Books
An imprint of
Hachette Children's Group
Part of Hodder and Stoughton
Carmelite House
50 Victoria Embankment
London EC4Y 0DZ

An Hachette UK Company
www.hachette.co.uk

www.hachettechildrens.co.uk

To daughters Lesley, Yansan, Kalera, grandson Marcus,
and to Reinhard Sander and Christopher Wrigley
for friendship that began the Lewes pathway

CONTENTS

When Questions Are Bliss

If I lie
on a page
am I a free word?

If I fly
in a cage
am I a trapped bird?

If I cry
with eyes of green
am I a weeping leaf?

Answers are folly
when questions are bliss
Without questions, do I exist?

Rooms

In the keeping room
we keep many things.
Exactly what, I'm not telling you.

In the sleeping room
naturally we sleep
and hope for a dream, perhaps two.

In the peeping room
we take a peep at life
while life peeps back out of the blue.

In the leaping room
we like to leap about.
It's known as doing the kangaroo.

In the heaping room
we heap our junk and stuff
for recycling into newer than new.

In the weeping room
we weep our hearts out
till the past has received its due.

That's when we return
to the keeping room
and keep our thoughts to ourselves.

The Rainmaker Danced

The rainmaker danced
the rainmaker danced
the rainmaker danced
and down came
the rains
in a flash.

'Bad news,' says the umpire.
'That's washed out the cricket match.'

Still the rainmaker danced
the rainmaker danced
the rainmaker danced
and the sky
surrendered its blue
to grey and more grey.

'There goes the barbecue!'
says the hostess.

'Lucky plants, rain's overdue,'
says the gardener.

Of course, it was nothing to do
with luck.

The rainmaker was none other
than a shape-shifting Duck.

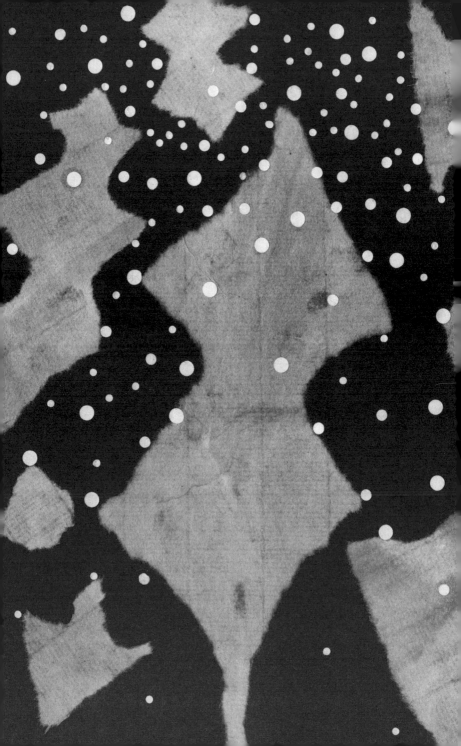

The Dew-Stealers

Who'd want to steal dew?
Maybe not me, maybe not you?
Then again, if you'd discovered
that dewdrops were heaven's pearls

(the precious spittle of the stars
according to that Roman Pliny)
yes, if dew meant liquid revenue
then even me, even you

might be tempted before sunrise
to creep up on unsuspecting grass
and steal from its store of gems
praying we're not caught on CCTV

sneaking off with dawn's treasury
still melting from our fingertips.

Hello Moon Hello Pig

Moon decided one night
to make a pig of herself.

So Moon shrugged off her bright yellow hood
and without saying goodbye to the stars
made her soundless way down sky's staircase
slipping into the first puddle's embrace.

It was hard work learning to drool and slobber
but Moon soon got the hang of rolling over
sidewards and bellywards in good old mud
until wallowing was easy as waxing and waning.

With more time and more practice
Moon got used to this form of mucky bathing.
In fact it became Moon's secret habit.
Surprise surprise she soon has herself a litter

of little potbellied curly-tailed moonlings.
And guess what? Moon showed her joy by grunting.

On The Run From Colours

Green misled me into the woods.
Blue tried to drown me in the sea.

White smothered me in balls of clouds.
Yellow caught me on a double yellow line.

Red greeted me with hands of blood.
Brown imprisoned my steps in clay.

Black offered to close my eyes in sleep.
But a nightmare got in the way.

Now even grey looks out to get me.
Fog, what are you? Friend or enemy?

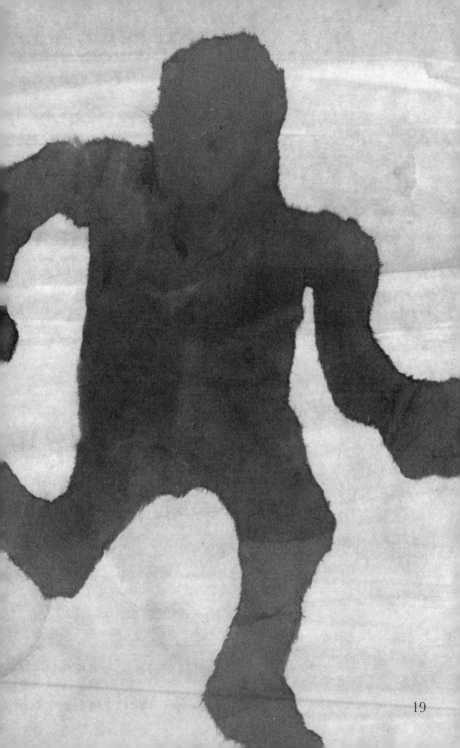

The Girl Who Married An Iron Stove

'Father, Father, O what have I done?
I've promised to marry an old iron stove
that helped me find my way out of the woods.'

'Daughter Daughter, I think I smell enchantment
when wedding bells are what make a stove content.
Go ask your mother for her humble opinion.'

'Don't worry, my child,' her mother declared.
'I'll see thee wed before I see my grave.
Shame it's an iron stove (not a microwave)!'

'But frogs have been kissed into princely hubbies.
Who knows what's to be of your bridegroom stove?
The strangest things happen in the name of love.'

'Your mother has spoken wisely,' the father agreed.
'A stove for a son-in-law will keep the neighbours guessing.
And a little stove for a grandchild will be our blessing.'

'Yes, we'll be the envy of the neighbourhood,'
nodded his wife. 'For when the winter takes its toll,
we shall have little grand stoves to warm our bones.'

The bride-to-be said not a word, simply smiled
as she scrubbed that stove with brush and with knife
until she heard a wee voice inside that iron prison

whispering: 'She who sets me free shall be my wife.
She who restores to me the lost light of day.
For I am not one formed of iron, but of clay.'

The Naming of Giants

A giant's name
should bludgeon the tongue
with a thundering sound –
a mouthful of syllables
to be savoured and gobbled.

Far better to be known as
a humungous blunderer
with a name like Blunderbore
or Blockerknob or Gogamog
than plain old Bill or Bob.

So says I, Gozzlemorebum the Gozzler,
son of Sizzlemorebum the Sizzler,
we whose ancient knuckles carved out hills
before the coming of peeny-puny mortals
with simpleton names like Jack and Jill.

Of Course I Believe In

Of course I believe in
Extra-terrestrials with
        extendable mandibles
the Yeti's mega footprint
        whose owner is untraceable
Nessie the monster who makes
        of a lake a habitable temple
Not to mention
the unicorn's singular
horn. Believe me, that was no fable.

It's not that I'm gullible
or even impressionable.
It's just that I respect the cred
        in incredible.

Seeking Answers

Do triangles
   ever get into a tangle
      when their sides meet their angles?

That fellow Pythagoras
   was he by any chance
      a pie enthusiast?

And is the Isosceles
   a rare form of eye disease?
      Someone answer please.

Though these questions of mine
   are mathematically pitched,
I'd say they'd be better answered
   by a patient psychiatrist.

Yu and Hi

And now beside Yellow River,
not far from shade of bamboo,
sits Chinese Empreror, Yu,
stroking chin as he ponders
mighty possible flood water.
'A dam!' thinks Emperor Yu
(who is also engineer).

As he wonders where to turn,
a voice says out of blue.
'Look on my back and learn.'
Who should this be but Turtle.
Not just any turtle, mind you.
But wise old black turtle named Hi,
ambassador of earth and sky.

Says divine Turtle to Emperor:
'As you are Yu and I am Hi,
I can see you are troubled
by thoughts of rising water.
But the dark markings of my shell
shall lighten your despair.
See the nine numbers on my back?
Therein lies a magic square.'

So by light of day, by lamp of night,
Emperor Yu studies those numbers all.
Adds them right to left, adds them left to right.
Adds them vertical, adds them horizontal.
Yes, Yu even adds them diagonal.
Yet answer, same, same. Always fifteen.
Why fifteen? What can this fifteen mean?

At long last, after much loss of sleep,
inspired Emperor Yu declares,
'Turtle's back shall be my maths teacher.
The dams and canals for my people
shall be laid like Turtle's magic square.
But to Yellow River, ever rising,
we must make fifteen offerings.'

Seagull Chant

Against a ship's
bulk of hull
Seagull Seagull
you dare your own
feathered hull
screech-beak-full
screech-beak-full.

Through storm and lull
by moon-pull
by sun-pull
Seagull Seagull
with you still around
the sea's never dull
the sea's never dull.

The Naming of a City

Ah Peritas, my Peritas,
cried Alexander the Great,
grieving for his faithful dog. Gone alas!

Peritas, who'd stood at his side
through battle thick and thin
of elephants and javelins.

Peritas, who with bark and bite
had braved the Persian cavalry,
never flinching from a fight.

Emperor Alexander, all tearful,
arranged a state funeral
for his long-time canine companion.

And in his sadness he declared:
'Though it is true all things come to pass,
I hereby name this city Peritas.'

But I should say enough of that.
Should I have cause to name a city,
I'll be naming it after my cat.

ΠΕΡΙΤΑΣ

33

Saluting Laika, the Sputnik Dog

Best first to launch a four-footer
into extra-terrestrial space
than to risk a two-footer
from what's known as the human race.

So up goes a husky mongrel
by the name of Laika.
But a capsule is no kennel
and soon Laika is a goner.

Alas, for Man's so-called best friend,
the end was Greekly tragic.
Laika snuffed it in a sputnik
with little time for last requests.

Near Moscow, Laika's monument
now rests for nation and for flag.
A canine cosmonauth and heroine
whose tail once knew how to wag.

The Countdown To Mars

'Mars, here I come,' said the scientist,
who was first among the chosen few.
'What old Galileo glimpsed was just a clue.
Landing on Mars, now that's a breakthrough!'

'Not a trip to be missed,' said the historian.
'To think an advanced civilisation might exist on Mars!
Wow! Fills me with mind boggling bliss!
I've lived my life for a moment like this.'

'Wouldn't miss Mars for the world,' said the surgeon.
And there sitting space-suited in the capsule
was one known far and wide as simply Fool.
How did he find himself in this gathering?

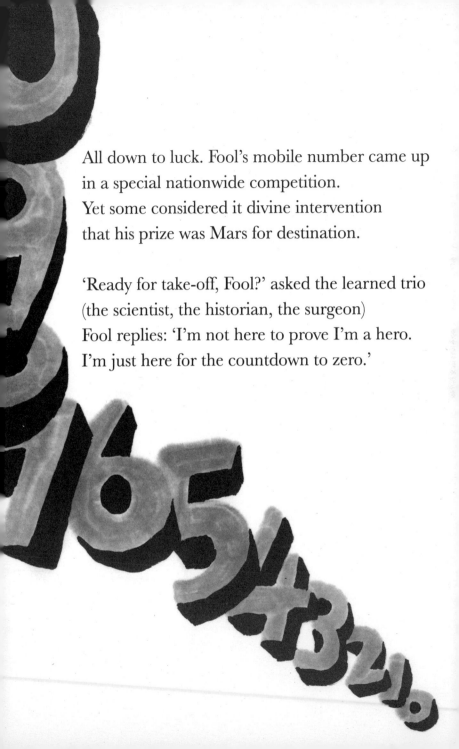

All down to luck. Fool's mobile number came up
in a special nationwide competition.
Yet some considered it divine intervention
that his prize was Mars for destination.

'Ready for take-off, Fool?' asked the learned trio
(the scientist, the historian, the surgeon)
Fool replies: 'I'm not here to prove I'm a hero.
I'm just here for the countdown to zero.'

GOVERNMENT WARNING!

YOU ARE ENTERING
A TICKLE-FREE ZONE.
ANY FUNNY BUSINESS
WITH THE FUNNY BONE
IS AGAINST THE LAW.
A TICKLE-INDUCED HA HA
OR UNAUTHORISED GUFFAW
IS STRICTLY FORBIDDEN
UNLESS BY WRITTEN AGREEMENT
BETWEEN THE TICKLER AND THE TICKLISH.
LAUGH AT YOUR OWN RISK.

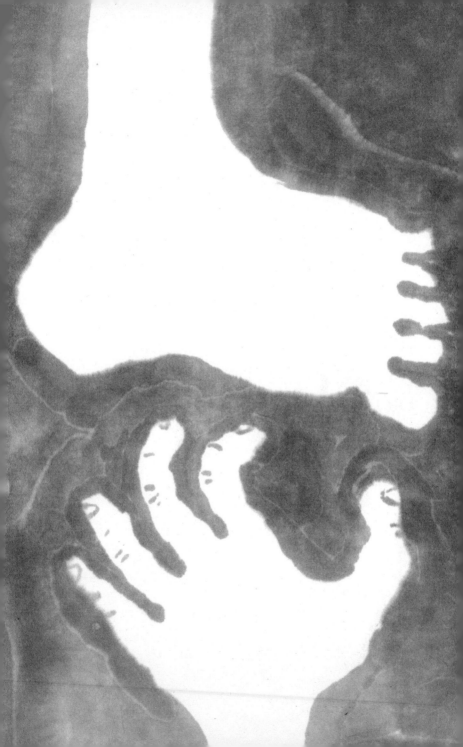

The Balloons And The Pins

The balloons and the pins
are at war again
and as usual the pins are winning –

the deflated bodies
of balloon poodles and bunnies
now lie in their colourful ruins.

But who'll spare a tear for fallen balloons?
Certainly not the triumphant pins.
Maybe the child with the helium eyes

still believing in the promise of birthdays
when next year's balloons regather and rise.

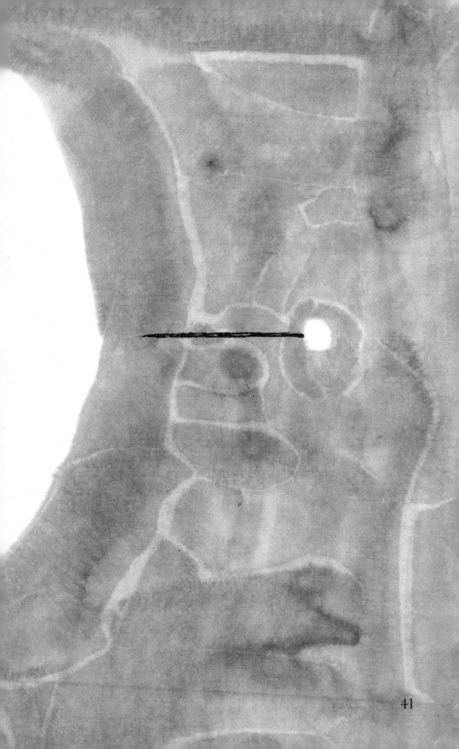

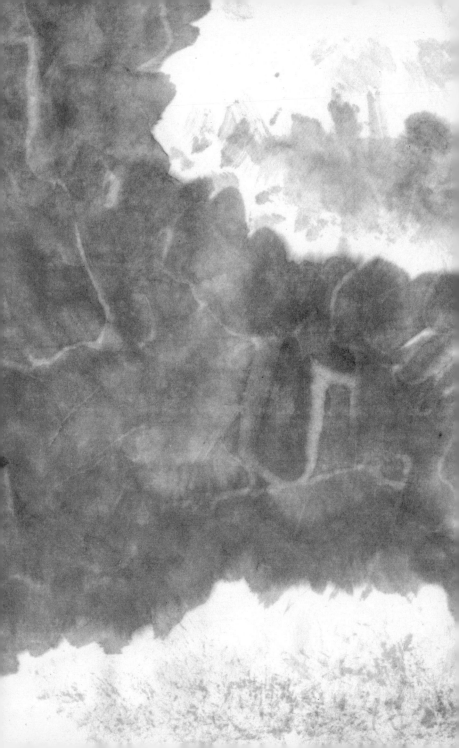

Progress

It takes time
to sling a stone
to fling a spear
to wield a club
to blow a dart
to shoot an arrow
to pull a pistol
to fire a canon

it takes a second
(maybe less)
to press
a button

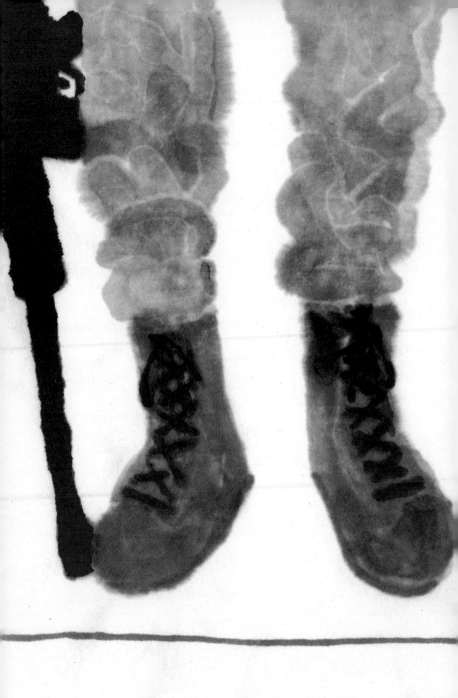

Line

Stand in line
they said
So he did.
Toe the line
they said
So he did.
Sign on
the dotted line
they said
So he did.

Then they sent him
to the frontline
where he learnt
of a thin line
between breathing
and not breathing.

A Single Cry

How strange to wake up
and find world peace has been declared.
You cannot believe your ears.
Has the breaking news on telly been broken far
too soon? Maybe.
But it's on twitter, it's on tweet.
War has been declared obsolete.
No more scenes of speechless desolation
and guns have suddenly gone dumb.
Bullets nestle in the recycling bin.
They can't wait for their new life to begin.
What's the reason for this overnight outbreak
of hugs, kisses, high fives, handshakes?
Don't ask me, mate, but the story goes,
people are now all friends, no more foes.
How will humans cope without enemies?
Well, might there be some in other galaxies?
So all around the globe you hear a single cry:
Unite against all those little green men from the sky.

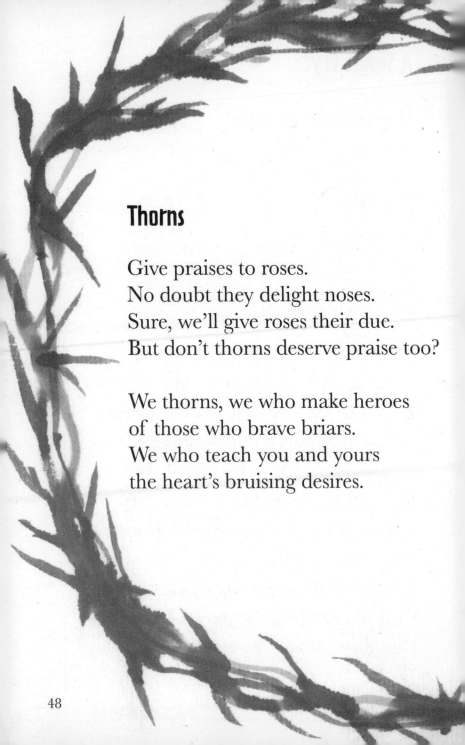

Thorns

Give praises to roses.
No doubt they delight noses.
Sure, we'll give roses their due.
But don't thorns deserve praise too?

We thorns, we who make heroes
of those who brave briars.
We who teach you and yours
the heart's bruising desires.

We thorns, we the ones who bled
from that holy crucified head.
When we thorns became a crown,
where were roses? Nowhere around.

Mosquito

My name is Mosquito.
It's true I'm no Firefly.
I just wouldn't know
how to do a sparkly fly.

This gift I've been denied.
Nor can I, like Butterfly,
become a pretty brooch
on a branch or leaf.

Mosquito's life on planet earth
is sadly all too brief,
(even one week, for what it's worth)
so we intend to make the most

of this very short lifespan
by feasting on the skin of Man.
(Of course, the skin of Woman too
will do nicely, thank you.)

An Off-The-Record Conversation

'Good morning, Butterfly Bush,
did you sleep well last night?'

'Unfortunately not.'

'Sorry to hear you didn't sleep well.
Was it all that raving late night music
that disturbed your leafy slumber?

Or was it that nasty thunder
and lightning from midnight till dawn?
The skies were really chucking it down.'

'Oh no, storms are no bother.
Lightning must do what lightning must do.
Never mind I lose a branch or two.

As for late-night foot-stomping parties,
they're the least of my worries.
I was up all night thinking of butterflies.'

'Butterflies? Why should Butterfly Bush
be losing sleep over butterflies?'

'Because these days they rarely visit me.
I feel like an abandoned granny.
And what's all this about endangered species?

Explain please.'

Three Old Mothers

Old Mother Frost is alive and well –
you can tell by the white on the ground
she's been shaking her feather bed
till snow feathers come tumbling down

Old Mother Thunder is in good spirits –
you can tell by the crackling in the air
and the rumbling in the distance
she's rocking away in her rocking chair

But Old Mother Ozone just sits and stares
into her ultra-violet mirror.
She's losing her hair layer by layer –
Cosmic doing? Or human error?

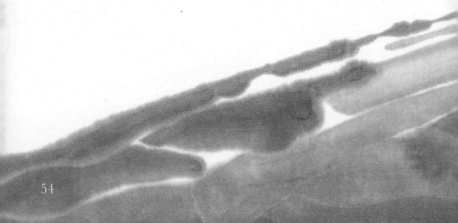

Praying Mantis

Cousin to grasshopper.
Accomplice of gardeners.

You there, at prayer on your knee,
yet armed with front leg choppers.
Unhappy at the end of horsefly or bee
that dares test your poised piety.

Praying Mantis – no stranger
to ancients of the Kalahari
where you are divine rain-bringer.
You who make the grass your altar.

Dear Flower

Dear Flower
Just writing to thank you
for your sudden bright smile
that puts the spring in my morning.
But I should also be thanking
those roots you keep out of sight,
those stems from which you take flight,
not to mention your fluttering
green companions, your leaves of course.
But how could I forget the clouds
that brought you the goodness of rain,
urging you towards blossom,

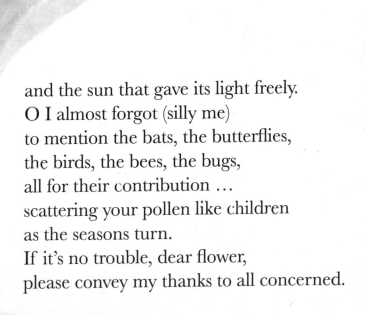

and the sun that gave its light freely.
O I almost forgot (silly me)
to mention the bats, the butterflies,
the birds, the bees, the bugs,
all for their contribution …
scattering your pollen like children
as the seasons turn.
If it's no trouble, dear flower,
please convey my thanks to all concerned.

Yours sincerely,
Traveller.

Goldfish
goldfish
which glass do you
prefer?
A bowl of glass
or a pond that ripples
when the winds pass?

Little bird
little bird
which do you prefer?
A house of wires
or a branch
that's a stage
for feathered choirs?

Red rose
red rose
which do you prefer?
A vase once used
to contain dry flowers
or a patch of ground
blooming with briars?

Putting such questions
to a goldfish
or a bird
or a rose
is pointless I suppose.

In The Land Where The Dead Bury The Dead

In the land where the dead bury the dead,
speeches are delivered without any words said.

Bones turn up in Sunday-best shrouds and tailored suits.
In church they sing hymns through mouths that stay mute.

They shed no tears yet their eyes are streaming wet.
And the dead are the first to pay their last respects.

They know when the time has come for the living to go
so they gather above to take new arrivals below.

The dead may be cold but they're not cold-hearted.
They always make room for the dear departed.

Later the dead will assemble over tea and biscuits
and liven themselves up with bits of underworld gossip.

But when it's time for me to pop my clogs, I trust
the dead will bury me without too much ceremony and fuss.

Pushing Up Daisies with Grandpa

Yes, lad, I'll pop me clogs.
I've had a long innings.
I'll kick the bucket.
Sure, I'll snuff it.

I'll cash in me chips.
I'll cross the river Styx.
I'll go Boothill, if I must.
Soon I'll bite the dust.

I'm in God's waiting room.
Departure lounge, if you prefer.
There I'll meet the Grim Reaper
as I make it to my Maker.

Time for me to sing me swan song.
Time to ring up me curtain down.
Pushing up daisies from the Beyond.
Pushing up daisies when I pass on.

Trust me, I'll not cease from toil
when I shove off this mortal coil.
No, I'll be pushing up daisies to the sky.
What's that, lad, did you say die?

Kangaroo Post

What impresses me most
        about you, Kangaroo

is not your hind-legged boogaloo
        or your forepaw boxer strokes

not your Down Under dreaming
        or your loose-limbed leaping.

No, what impresses me most
        is your miracle envelope –

that pouch through which you post
        your first-class babies to the future.

Dinosaur Meets Electronic Mouse

A dinosaur, just back from extinction,
had centuries of techno inventions to think on.
Still old Brontosaurus kept his blinkers on
as he surveyed the digital revolution.

Brontosaurus stared at electronic mouse.
Electronic mouse stared back at Brontosaurus.
Neither of them had got the other sussed.
Both creatures, you could say, were nonplussed.

Electronic mouse said: 'Don't come too close.
I wouldn't want you to catch my virus.'
Dino replied: 'The last mouse I saw… let me think …
was the day before I found myself extinct.

Of course, that was millennia before your time
when mice like you possessed what's called a squeak.'
Electronic mouse burrowed into her screen and sighed:
'This Dino has some way to go to becoming a Geek!'

Switched On Without
Final Reminders

Fire-beetles
have their underbelly sensors
for sensing fires miles away

human beetles
also have their smoke detectors
for detecting smoke night or day.

Arctic foxes
have their fur insulators
for keeping winter's bite at bay

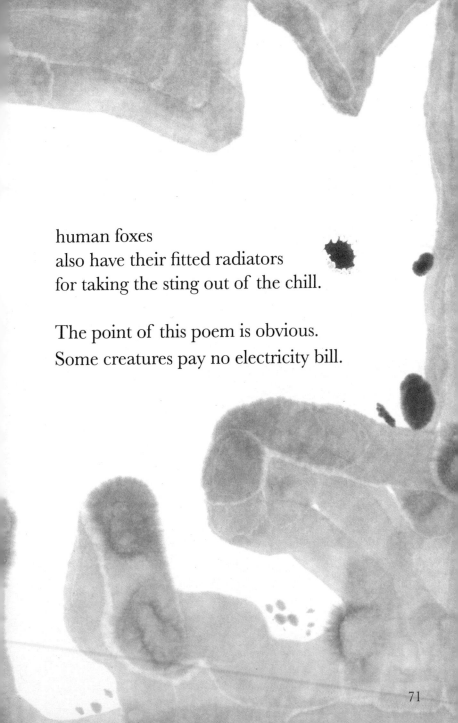

human foxes
also have their fitted radiators
for taking the sting out of the chill.

The point of this poem is obvious.
Some creatures pay no electricity bill.

Lost Sheep

I like being the lost sheep.
I don't want to be found
I like being a frisking-free sheep
In unfamiliar ground

I like being the lost sheep
with my head in the clouds
It's liberating to bleat
far from the gullible crowd

I won't return to the fold
I rejoice in being lost,
Who wants to be served cold
as main course with mint sauce?

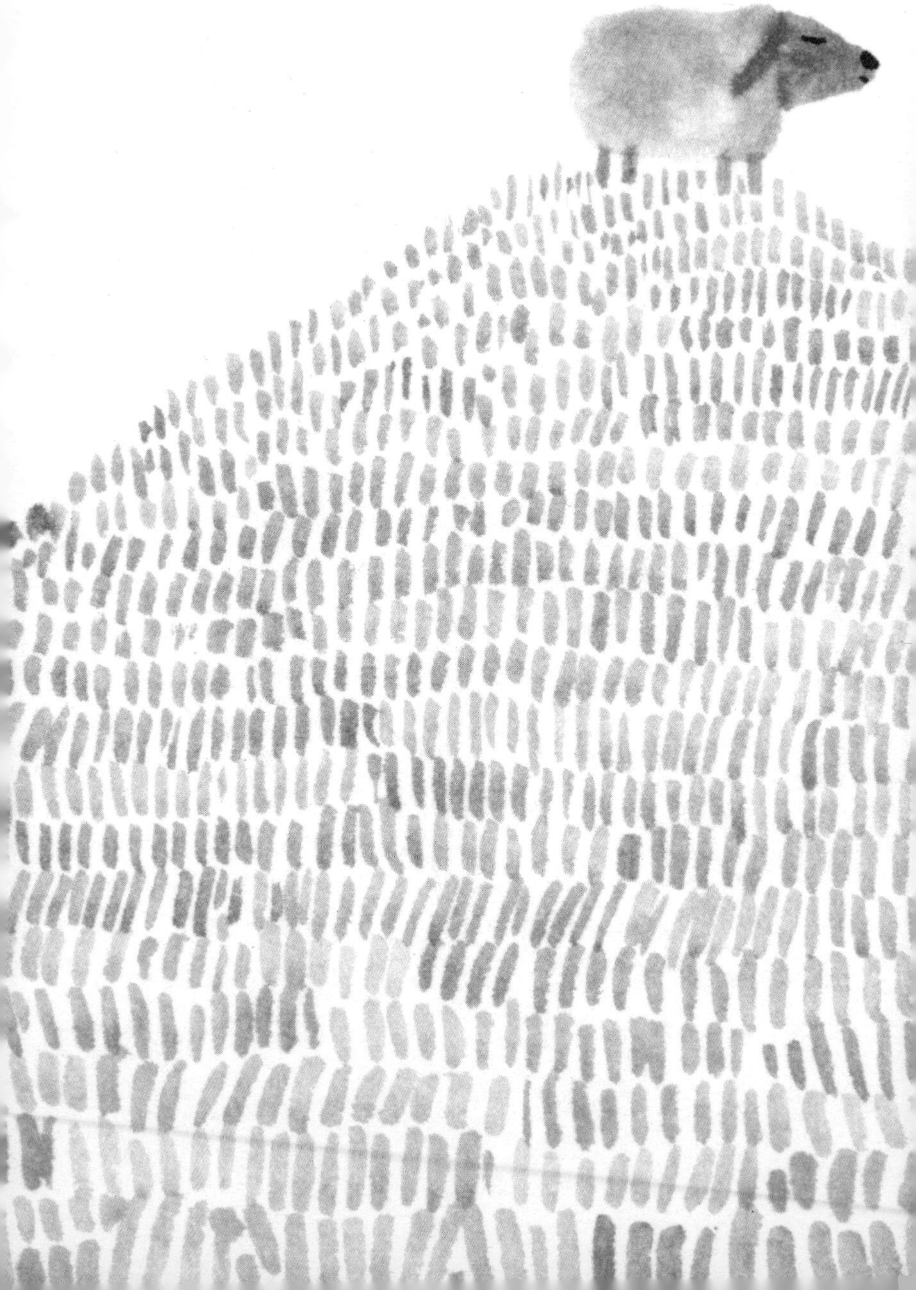

By Their Fruits Ye Shall Know Them

If humans and animals can be compared:
say a hairy grandpa to a cuddly panda
say a limbo dancer to a wriggly cobra
say a full-o-beans toddler to a frisky hare

then why can't people and fruits be paired
(no pun intended)? So those I find easy
to get along with, I'll call banana-breezy.
Not like those who are pineapple-pricklies.

Yes, the world is full of all fruit-types.
Some are green yet act like they're ripe.
And some look downright rotten outside –
Until you discover their inside.

Then of course you have those who show
the world a tough coconut exterior –
never wanting to appear a softie.
Coconuts with a deep down heart of strawberry.

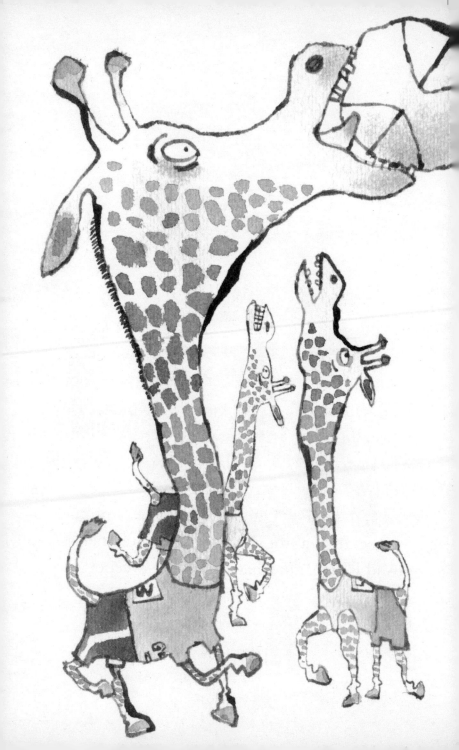

The Four Footed Olympians

If our four footed-friends competed in sport,
we'd surely see some fit females and blokes.
Giraffe's height would rule the basketball court.
Hippo's weight would boss any wrestling ring.
Leaping Hare a certain gold for triple jumping,
Kangaroo Rat a world record-breaking hurdler.
Polar Bear, of course, born to be a skier.
Don't write off Otter, synchronised swimmer.
Cheetah at a trot would lead the 100 metres.
And Rhino, ah, what a midfield sweeper!
But pity the poor penalty shooter
who must face Octopus for a goalkeeper.
O pity even more the ill-timed referee
who waves a red card to Tiger in a jersey.

The Tomato Says I Do

Who'll be Frankenstein's bride?
Not I
says the corn.
I'm already engaged to the sun.

Who'll be Frankenstein's bride?
Not I
says the wheat.
The wind is my devoted husband.

Who'll be Frankenstein's bride?
Not I
says the mushroom.
Can't you see I'm a fairy's footstool?

Who'll be Frankenstein's bride?
Not I
says the grape.
I'm already wedded to the vine.

Very well, I'll be Frankenstein's bride
says the tomato.
I'll walk him down the aisle

providing of course
that his blushes
were genetically modified.

The Bi-phibians Are Coming

What gives a cow
      Cow-dentity?
Is it the horn
or the rolling laidback moo?

What gives an owl
      Owl-dentity?
Is it the hoot
or the night-time point of view?

What gives a dog
      Dog-dentity?
Is it the bark
or the welcome wag of tail?

What gives a cat
      Cat-dentity
Is it the purr
or the caterwauling wail?

What gives a bee
      Bee-dentity?

Is it the buzz
or the shimmer of wing?

What gives a fish
        Fish-dentity?
Is it the scale
or the fingerprint fin?

What gives me
        I-dentity
Is it the tone of skin
or the colour of speech?

What makes the you in me reach
out to the me somewhere in you?
Since I'm the offspring of sea and land
then that must make me Bi-phibian

Delighted, my friend, to meet you.
Do you by chance tick Bi-phibian too?

Taking Sides

What religion
does the rain follow?
It descends with little
thought of litany
or bended knee,
yet rain fills the air
with drops of prayer.

Which language
does the thunder speak?
Its expressive claps
need no translator
for all who take shelter
from a storm's rolling outburst.
Thunder respects no borders.

And those birds
that are morning's chorus?
Whose side are they on?
Are they for us or for them?
Those birds that warble
the same anthem
for enemy as well as friend?

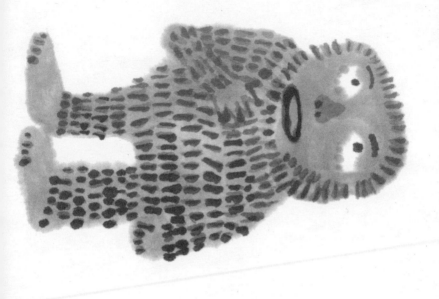

Among The Hairyboos And Smoothyboos

The Hairyboos were hairy, the Smoothyboos smooth.
But they lived side by side and were never rude.
Strangely, their language had no word for hate,
they called a stranger like myself *afar-heart-mate*.
These two undiscovered races spoke the same tongue.
Their national anthem sounds fun (even in translation).

'Hairyboo, Smoothyboo, we same people.
Two different rivers, one ripple.
Forward Hairyboo, Forward Smoothyboo,
Ever onward, ever tickety-boo.'

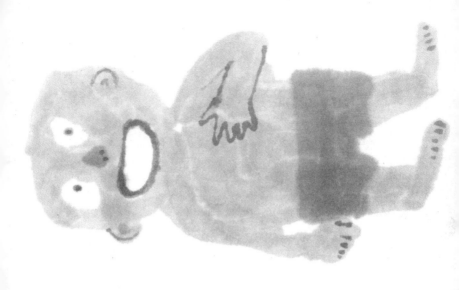

And you'd think they sing standing to attention.
But no, they sing their anthem lying down
in what's known as the circle of one heartbeat,
while the men and women stare at each other's feet.
This is an ancient tradition (or so I've been told)
for they say to ponder the feet is to ponder the soul.

The Hairyboos are worshippers of bristles and fur,
and treat as sacred the coconut's hairy shell.
The Smoothyboos, on the other hand, pray to pebbles.
And in every egg or ball they see a miracle.
These almost extinct tribes have an old expression:
If you don't have an enemy, why invent one?

The Encounter

How lovely to meet a man
who said he'd come from nowhere.
I'd always been fed the view
that everyone comes from somewhere.

He greeted me, as the locals do,
with a down-to-earth Goodie day.
He said he'd just arrived from nowhere
and did not intend to stay.

Just passing through, just passing through.
Can't wait to get back to nowhere.
Don't know how you folks from somewhere
can cope with being in one hemisphere.

Homo Ambi-thumb-trous

In times when eyes stare
into eyes of mobile phones
and ears imprison ears
in their *don't-talk-to-me zones*

I've seen folk texting
with their left thumb
I've seen folk texting
with their right thumb.

Now don't get me wrong,
I'm not hi-tech dumb.
But those texting with two thumbs
(at one go) leave me spellbound.

Roll over *Homo Erectus.*
Make way for Homo Ambi-thumb-trous.

Also available:

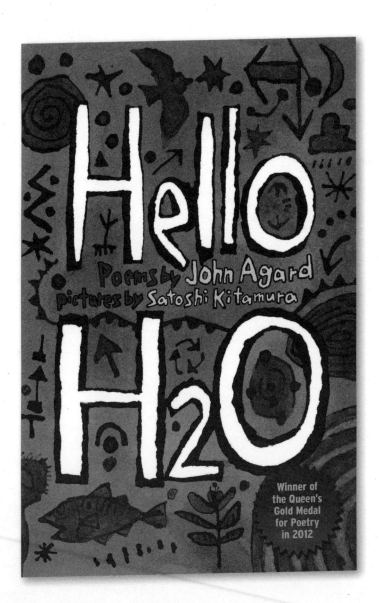